Olive A. Wadsworth

Over in the Meadow

A Counting-Out Rhyme

Pictures by
Mary Maki Rae

PUFFIN BOOKS

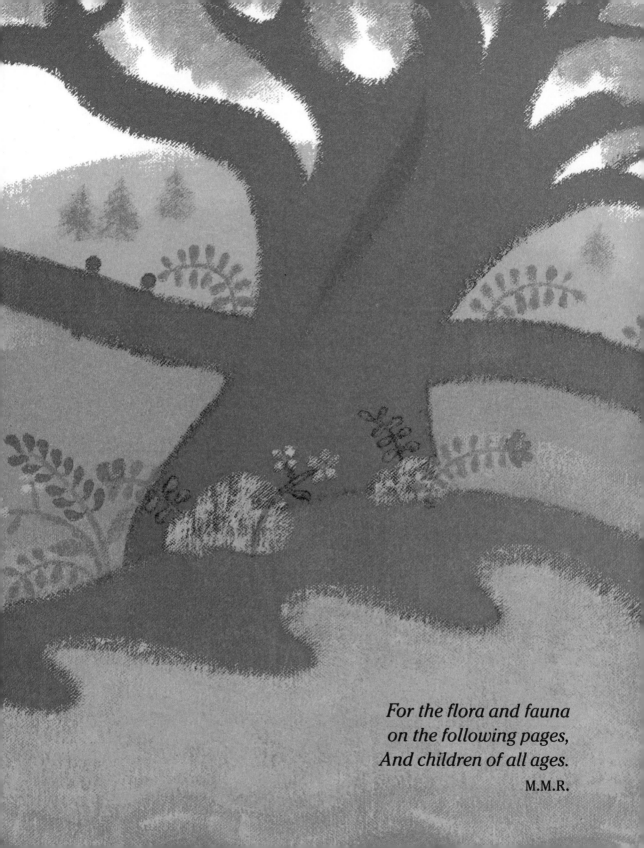

*For the flora and fauna
on the following pages,
And children of all ages.*

M.M.R.

PUFFIN BOOKS
Published by the Penguin Group
Penguin Books USA Inc.
375 Hudson Street, New York, New York 10014, U.S.A.
Penguin Books Ltd, 27 Wrights Lane, London W8 5TZ, England
Penguin Books Australia Ltd, Ringwood, Victoria, Australia
Penguin Books Canada Ltd, 10 Alcorn Avenue, Suite 300, Toronto, Ontario, Canada MV4 3B2
Penguin Books (N.Z.) Ltd, 182-190 Wairau Road, Auckland 10, New Zealand
Penguin Books Ltd, Registered Offices: Harmondsworth, Middlesex, England

First published by Viking Penguin Inc. 1985
Published in Picture Puffins 1986
10 9 8 7 6
Illustrations copyright © Mary Maki Rae, 1985
All rights reserved

Library of Congress Cataloging in Publication Data
Wadsworth, Olive A   Over in the meadow.
Summary: Traditional rhyme about different animals
living in the meadow introduces the numbers one through ten.
1. Nursery rhymes. 2. Children's poetry. [1. Nursery rhymes. 2. Counting]
I. Rae, Mary Maki, ill. II. Title. PZ8.3.W132Ov 1986   398′.8   85-43386 ISBN 0-14-050606-3

Over in the meadow in the sand in the sun
Lived an old mother turtle and her little turtle one.
Dig, said the mother. *We dig,* said the one.
So they dug all day in the sand in the sun.

Over in the meadow where the stream runs blue
Lived an old mother fish and her little fishes two.
Swim, said the mother. *We swim*, said the two.
So they swam all day where the stream runs blue.

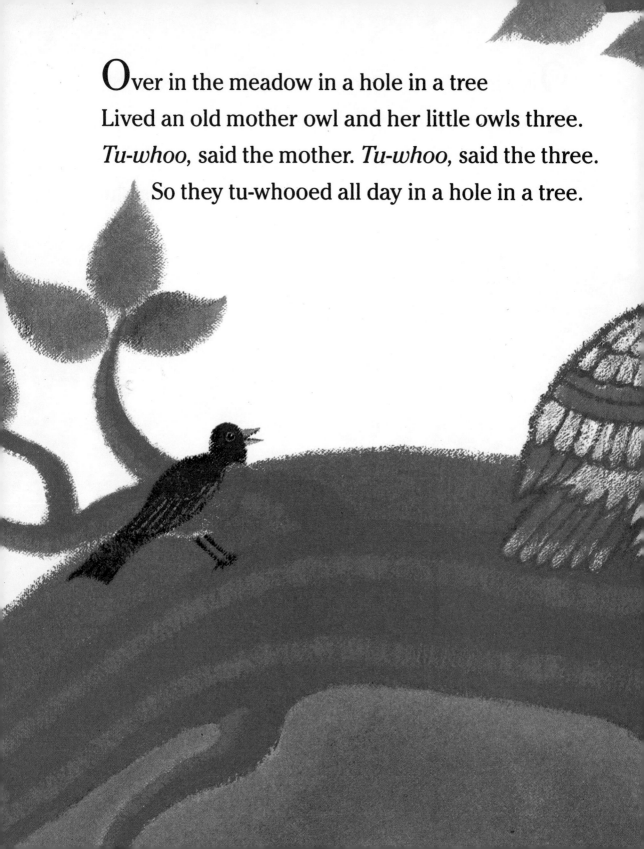

Over in the meadow in a hole in a tree
Lived an old mother owl and her little owls three.
Tu-whoo, said the mother. *Tu-whoo*, said the three.
So they tu-whooed all day in a hole in a tree.

Over in the meadow by the old barn door
Lived an old mother rat and her little ratties four.
Gnaw, said the mother. *We gnaw*, said the four.
So they gnawed all day by the old barn door.

Over in the meadow in a snug beehive
Lived an old mother bee and her little bees five.
Buzz, said the mother.
We buzz, said the five.
So they buzzed all day
in a snug beehive.

Over in the meadow in a nest built of sticks
Lived an old mother crow and her little crows six.
Caw, said the mother. *We caw*, said the six.
So they cawed all day in a nest built of sticks.

Over in the meadow where the grass grows so even
Lived an old mother frog and her little froggies seven.
Jump, said the mother. *We jump*, said the seven.
So they jumped all day where the grass grows so even.

Over in the meadow by the old mossy gate
Lived an old mother lizard and her little lizards eight.
Bask, said the mother. *We bask*, said the eight.
So they basked all day by the old mossy gate.

Over in the meadow by the old Scotch pine
Lived an old mother duck and her little ducks nine.
Quack, said the mother.
We quack, said the nine.
So they quacked all day
by the old Scotch pine.

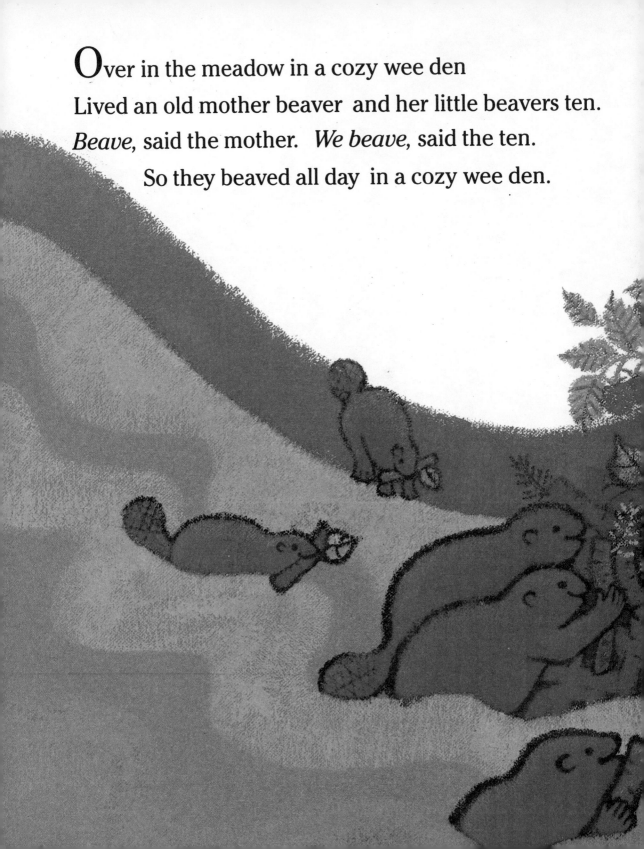

Over in the meadow in a cozy wee den
Lived an old mother beaver and her little beavers ten.
Beave, said the mother.   *We beave*, said the ten.
So they beaved all day in a cozy wee den.

3

4

6

9 10